Contents

A Note About the Author and His Stories

Montague Rhodes James (1862–1936) was a scholar who wrote many books on history and languages. He also wrote many famous ghost stories. He read these stories to his friends at King's College, Cambridge University.

Many of the people in the stories have plenty of money and do not need to work. They live in large houses and have servants to look after them. Many of them like to travel. All of them are interested in books.

These people lived in the same way that M. R. James lived. But life for ordinary people was very different.

As you read these stories, think about M. R. James. He read these stories at Christmas. He sat in a room lit by candles. Outside it was dark and cold. The gentlemen listened to James reading. They smoked cigars and drank brandy.

After you have read the story, it will be time to go to bed. But don't turn out the light straight away. Something may be waiting for you, in the dark!

ROOM 13

Viborg is a city in Denmark. It is an old city, but it has only a few old buildings. A great fire destroyed most of the old town in 1726.

Mr Anderson was writing a book on the history of Denmark. He went to Viborg in 1891. He wanted to study the history of the town.

He stayed in an old building in Viborg – The Golden Lion Inn. The inn was nearly 350 years old.

Anderson asked the landlord for a large room. The landlord of The Golden Lion showed him two rooms – room number 12 and room number 14. There were three large windows in each room. The windows looked onto the street. Anderson chose room number 12.

In the evening, Anderson went downstairs for supper. He saw a blackboard. The names of all the guests were written on the blackboard. Anderson saw that the inn was full. There were no empty rooms. Anderson noticed that there was no room number 13.

Thirteen is an unlucky number. Many people do not want to stay in a room with an unlucky number.

When Anderson went upstairs to bed, he tried to unlock his door. It did not open. Then he saw that he had made a mistake. It was the wrong room. The number on the door was number 13.

He heard someone moving inside the room.

'I'm very sorry,' he said and went to the door of room number 12.

Perhaps the servants sleep in room 13, Anderson thought. He decided to ask the landlord about it the next day.

Anderson lit the oil-lamp and looked round. Room number 12 looked smaller by lamplight. Anderson was tired. He went to bed.

In the morning, Anderson went to the Town Hall. He wanted to study the town records. Anderson read many very old papers. The oldest records were from the sixteenth century.

There were some letters from the Bishop of Viborg, dated 1560. The Bishop had owned three or four houses in the city. He had rented a house to a man called Nicolas Francken.

The townspeople of Viborg did not like Nicolas Francken. Some people wrote to the Bishop to say that Francken was a bad man. They said that Francken was a magician. They wanted Francken to leave the city.

The Bishop said that Nicolas Francken had done nothing wrong. He did not believe that Francken was a magician.

It was time for the Town Hall to close. As Anderson was leaving, the town clerk spoke to him.

'I see you are reading about the Bishop and Nicolas Francken,' the clerk said. 'I am interested in them. But I do not know where Francken lived. Many of the town records were burnt in the great fire of 1726.'

Anderson thanked the clerk and went back to The Golden Lion. He wanted to ask the landlord about room number 13, but the landlord was busy.

Anderson went upstairs and stopped outside the door of number 13. He heard someone inside the room. The person was walking around and talking in a strange voice.

Anderson went to his own room. He decided that number 12 was too small. He decided to ask the landlord for a large room. Also, he was angry because his suitcase was

6

missing. It had been on a table beside the wall. Both the table and the suitcase had disappeared. Perhaps the landlord had moved the suitcase to a store-room. Anderson wanted it back.

It was too late to call the landlord. Anderson went to the window and lit a cigarette.

He looked out of the window. There was a tall house on the opposite side of the street. The lamp was behind him. He saw his shadow on the wall of the house opposite. The person in room 13 was also standing at the window. Anderson saw a second shadow on the wall of the house opposite.

This second shadow was strange. The person in room 13 was wearing a tall, pointed hat. Also, the light from room 13 was red. The light was the colour of blood.

Anderson opened the window and put his head outside. He tried to see the person in the next room. He saw the sleeve of a long, white coat – that was all. The person in room 13 suddenly moved away from the window. The red light went out.

Anderson finished his cigarette. He left the ashtray on the window ledge. Then he turned out the lamp and went to bed.

Next morning, the maid brought hot water to the room. Anderson woke up and remembered his suitcase.

'Where is my suitcase, please?' he asked.

The maid laughed and pointed. The suitcase was on the table beside the wall. It was exactly where Anderson had left it.

He noticed another strange thing. His ashtray was on the *middle* window-ledge. He clearly remembered smoking his cigarette by the end window – next to number 13.

He finished dressing and decided to visit his neighbour in

He tried to see the person in the next room.

room 13. He was surprised when he went to the door of the next room. The next room was number 14! Anderson was frightened. Was he going mad?

After breakfast, he went to the Town Hall and read more of the old papers. He found only one more letter from the Bishop about Nicolas Francken. A group of townspeople had tried to make Francken leave Viborg. They had gone to Francken's house, but Francken had disappeared. The Bishop wrote that no one knew where Flancken had gone. That was the end of the matter.

That evening, Anderson spoke to the landlord of The Golden Lion Inn.

'Why is there no room 13 in the inn?' he asked.

'Many people won't sleep in a room number 13,' the landlord replied. 'They say it's unlucky.'

'Then who is in your room number 13?' asked Anderson.

'There isn't a room number 13,' the landlord said. 'Your room is next to room number 14.'

'Of course,' said Anderson. 'I must have made a mistake. Would you like to come up to number 12 for a glass of brandy and a cigar?'

'I'd like to very much,' said the landlord.

They went upstairs together. They went past room number 10 and room number 11 to reach number 12.

The landlord looked at the inside of number 12.

'This room looks very small,' he said.

Anderson poured two glasses of brandy. Both men lit cigars.

Anderson opened the window to let out the smoke. There was a red light and a shadow on the wall of the house opposite. The light came from number 13. The shadow was dancing wildly, but there was no noise.

Anderson sat down to drink his brandy. He wanted to tell the landlord about the strange things he had seen. Suddenly a terrible noise came from the next room.

'Is that a cat?' asked Anderson. 'Or is there a madman in the room next door?'

'It's Mr Jensen,' said the landlord. 'He often stays in room 14. The poor man must be ill.'

A loud knock sounded on the door of Anderson's room. Suddenly a man opened the door and came in.

'Please stop that terrible noise,' the man said.

'Mr Jensen!' the landlord said. 'We thought you were making the noise!'

The three men looked at each other for a moment. Then they went out quickly into the corridor. The noise was coming from the door of room number 13!

The landlord banged on the door and turned the handle. The door was locked.

'I'll bring men to break the door down,' the landlord shouted and ran down the stairs.

Jensen and Anderson stood outside number 13. The noise inside the room became louder and wilder.

'I want to tell you something strange,' Jensen said to Anderson. 'My room has three windows in the day and only two at night. Perhaps you think I am mad?'

'Good Lord! My room is the same!' said Anderson. 'My room looks smaller at night than during the day.'

The door of number 13 opened suddenly and an arm came out. The arm was thin and covered in grey hairs. The fingernails were long and dirty.

Anderson shouted and pulled Jensen away from the door. The arm disappeared and the door closed. The sound of mad laughter came from number 13.

The landlord brought two men up the stairs. The men had axes in their hands. They swung their axes against the door of number 13.

Suddenly the men cried out and dropped their axes. They had hit a wall. The door of number 13 had disappeared!

In the morning, workmen pulled up the floor between rooms 12 and 14.

Under the floor they found a box. There were old papers inside the box. Anderson thought that the papers belonged to Nicolas Francken – the man who had disappeared in 1560.

No one was able to read the writing on the papers. It was in a strange language. The writing was brown. The ink looked old. But Anderson did not think it was ink. He thought the papers were written in blood!

THE WHISTLE

Burnstow is a small seaside town. It is a busy town in summer. But it is a quiet place for the rest of the year. In spring and autumn, only a few people go there. They go to Burnstow to play golf.

Professor Parkins went to Burnstow in the spring of 1902. He stayed at a small inn called The Globe. The Globe Inn was very near the sea.

There were only two rooms for guests at the inn. There was a guest in one of the rooms so the Professor had to stay in the other. The landlord took the Professor upstairs to the room.

The landlord unlocked the door and showed the Professor the room.

'This is the room, sir,' he said. 'There are two beds. Both of them are comfortable. You can choose the bed you want. There's a good view of the sea from the window.'

Professor Parkins looked out of the window. The beach was only a hundred yards away. The sea looked grey and cold. Then the Professor noticed that there were no curtains on the window.

'Landlord,' he said. 'There are no curtains on the window.'

'I'm very sorry, sir,' said the landlord. 'I'll tell the servant to put them up.'

That afternoon, Professor Parkins met the other guest. His name was Colonel Wilson. They decided to play golf together.

The two men walked along the road to the golf-course. They talked about their lives and their work. Colonel Wilson had been an army officer in India. He had lived in

India for many years.

'I am an archeologist,' said Professor Parkins. 'I study history by digging up old buildings.'

'Are there any old buildings here in Burnstow?' asked the Colonel.

'I believe there was an old church near the golf-course,' said the Professor. 'But it was pulled down in the fourteenth century.'

'Why?' asked the Colonel. 'It's unusual to pull down a church, isn't it?'

'Yes,' said the Professor. 'I don't know why it was pulled down. That's why I want to look for it. I want to find the place where the church stood.'

They played golf for most of the afternoon.

'Shall we go back to the inn for a drink before supper?' the Colonel asked.

'I will see you at the inn in half an hour,' the Professor said. 'First, I will look for the old church.'

'Don't be late,' said the Colonel. 'It will be dark soon.'

The Colonel walked along the road towards the inn. The Professor walked towards the beach. He looked at the ground carefully.

There were many large, grey stones near the beach. The stones were covered with grass. They were placed in the shape of a circle.

The Professor touched a stone with his foot. The stone moved. There was a hole underneath the stone.

Professor Parkins looked into the hole. It was dark in the hole and he could not see anything. So he lit a match. The wind blew the match out.

He put his hand into the hole. The hole was empty.

No – he was wrong. His fingers touched something made

of metal. He pulled it out of the hole. It was a piece of metal about four inches long. It was old and dirty. He put it in his pocket.

The wind from the sea was cold and the sky was cloudy. It was getting dark. Professor Parkins decided to walk back to the inn.

It was a short walk along the beach to the inn, but there were high breakwaters on the beach. The Professor climbed over each of the breakwaters slowly. It was hard work. He stopped to rest.

He looked back and saw someone about a hundred yards behind him. The other person stopped. It was getting dark, so the Professor could not see clearly. He could not see what the other person looked like. A black figure on the beach was watching him. Was it a man or a woman? Or was it something else?

The Professor suddenly felt afraid. He did not want to meet this strange figure on the dark beach. He thought that the figure was following him. He started to run, but the sand was soft and deep and the breakwaters were high. He felt he was running in a dream.

At last he reached the inn. He looked round. There was no one behind him on the dark beach. He was cold and tired and very glad to go into the warm inn.

The Colonel was waiting for him. They ate supper together and talked about golf. Then the Professor went upstairs to his room.

As he took off his jacket, he remembered the piece of metal in his pocket. He took it out and looked at it by candlelight. It was a very old whistle.

He tried to blow the whistle. No noise came out. The whistle was full of dirt.

The Professor took out a small pocket-knife. He went to the window to clean the dirt out of the whistle.

He saw that there were still no curtains on the window. He opened the window and looked out. The night was dark. There was no moon. But the Professor thought there was someone standing on the beach.

He cleaned the whistle quickly then went back to the candle. Now he could see marks on the whistle. The marks were letters – QUIS EST ISTE QUI VENIT.

Latin! the Professor thought. "Quis est iste qui venit" means – "Who is this who is coming?"

The Professor tried to blow the whistle.

No one will come, he thought. But he put the whistle to his lips and blew.

The sound of the whistle was clear and high. It was a sad sound. Suddenly the wind blew strongly through the open window. The candle went out. The Professor was surprised and frightened. He stood in the dark listening to the wind.

He walked slowly across the room. He closed the window. Still the wind blew. It blew around the inn making a terrible noise.

The Professor relit the candle with a match. He felt tired and cold. He put the whistle on a table and undressed. Then he got into one of the beds and blew out the candle.

When he closed his eyes, he dreamt he was on the beach. He saw the high breakwaters. It was dark but he saw every thing clearly.

He saw someone running. Every few seconds, the man looked behind him. The man was frightened and tired. He climbed over each breakwater more slowly. Finally, he fell on the sand and lay still. He had a look of terror on his face.

Behind the man, someone or something was moving very

quickly. It came nearer and nearer. It was a strange black figure. It came closer and closer to the man who lay on the beach. It stopped. And then it jumped straight towards the man.

Professor Parkins opened his eyes. He was too afraid to see what happened next. Every time he closed his eyes, he had the same dream.

At last, he reached for his matches and lit the candle. Something moved on the floor under his bed. He thought it was a mouse.

The Professor was not able to sleep again. When morning

came, he went downstairs for breakfast.

'You don't look well,' the Colonel said. 'A game of golf will make you feel better.'

'Yes,' said the Professor. 'I need some fresh air.'

After breakfast, the Professor went upstairs to get his hat. The servant was cleaning his room.

'Good morning, sir,' the girl said. 'It was cold and windy last night. Would you like another blanket for your bed?'

'Yes, please,' said the Professor.

'Which bed shall I put it on, sir?' asked the girl.

'The one I slept in,' said the Professor.

'But you slept in both beds, sir,' said the girl. 'I put clean sheets on both beds.'

'Did I?' said the Professor. 'Put a blanket on the bed in the corner.'

As soon as the girl had finished, the Professor left the room. He locked the door and put the key in his pocket.

He met the Colonel downstairs. They walked along the road to the golf-course.

'It was very windy last night,' said the Colonel. 'When there was a bad storm in India, we said that someone had whistled for the wind.'

'Well,' said the Professor slowly. 'I blew a whistle last night and the wind came soon afterwards.'

'How very strange,' said the Colonel. 'Tell me, what kind of whistle was it?'

The Professor told the Colonel about the whistle. He told him how he had found it. He told him that he had cleaned it and blown it. He did not tell him that he had stayed awake all night.

The Colonel listened to the story but said nothing. They played golf until late in the afternoon.

They walked back along the road to the inn. The Professor did not want to walk back along the beach.

They were very near the inn when a boy came running towards them. He ran straight into the Colonel and fell over.

'What's the matter?' the Colonel asked angrily. 'Look where you're going!'

The boy was very frightened. The Colonel spoke to him again, 'Who are you running away from?'

'The thing in the window,' the boy answered. He was crying.

'What thing?' the Colonel asked. 'Come and show us.'

The boy took them to the front of The Globe Inn. He pointed up to a window.

'It was up there, sir,' he said. 'It was waving at me. But it was a horrible thing, sir. I don't think it was alive!'

'Don't be afraid,' the Colonel said. 'It was someone trying to frighten you. Go home and forget about it.'

The Colonel looked at the Professor.

'That's the window of your room isn't it?' he asked.

'Yes,' said the Professor. 'There's something strange going on. Will you come upstairs with me?'

The two men went upstairs together. The Professor's room was locked. He opened the door with his key.

Inside the room, one of the beds was untidy. A sheet lay on the floor by the window. The Professor called the servant.

'Who has been in my room?' asked the Professor.

'No one, sir,' the servant replied. 'There are only two keys to this room. You have one and the landlord has the other.'

The Professor went to find the landlord.

'I didn't go into your room while you were out, sir,' said the landlord.

The Professor and the Colonel ate supper together.

'I can't understand it,' said the Professor. 'How can someone have gone into a locked room?'

'Show me the whistle you told me about,' said the Colonel.

The Professor showed it to him.

'What will you do with it?' asked the Colonel.

'I shall put it in a museum,' said the Professor.

'Throw it into the sea,' said the Colonel. 'I'm going to bed. Call me if you need me in the night.'

Professor Parkins went to his room. The night was clear and the moon was full. Bright moonlight shone through the window. There were still no curtains. The Professor was angry.

The moonlight will shine through the window and keep me awake, he thought. He decided to hang a sheet over the window. He took a sheet from the empty bed and hung it on the curtain rail. Then he got into his own bed and went to sleep.

He did not sleep for long. Bright moonlight woke him up. The sheet was no longer over the window. A noise came from the empty bed. The Professor looked across the room.

Suddenly a figure sat up on the other bed. The Professor was so surprised that he jumped out of his own bed. He stood by the window. There was moonlight, but he could not see the figure on the other bed clearly. It was covered with a sheet.

The figure stood up. It stood between the Professor and the door. Its arms were spread out. It was searching for the Professor with its fingers!

The figure stood up. Its arms were spread out.

The figure jumped on the Professor's empty bed. It moved slowly over the pillow. The Professor shivered with fear.

Then the figure got off the bed and moved towards the window. In the bright moonlight, the Professor could see its face under the sheet. It was very old and very horrible.

The Professor opened the window and shouted for help. The figure under the sheet jumped forward. Its hands went over the Professor's mouth.

The Professor tried to get away. He was about to fall out of the window when a hand pulled him back.

It was the Colonel. There was no one else in the room. A sheet from the bed lay on the floor by the window.

Next morning, the Colonel and the Professor went down to the beach. The Colonel took the strange whistle and threw it into the sea.

'Things like this sometimes happen in India,' the Colonel said. 'I don't think the figure can hurt you. It can only frighten you.'

Professor Parkins is still afraid of curtains that move in the wind. He also sleeps without sheets on his bed.

THE MESSAGE OF DEATH

> The Museum Society,
> London
>
> 20th April 1900
>
> Dear Mr. Karswell,
>
> I have received your letter of 18th April. The Museum Society is **not** interested in your book on magic. I told you this in my earlier letters. Please do not write to me again. I will not reply to any more of your letters.
>
> Yours sincerely,
> C. Dunning (Secretary)

Mr Dunning finished writing and signed the letter. Karswell had written a book on magic. He wanted to give it to the Museum Society to keep in their library. Dunning was the secretary of the Society. He thought that the book was nonsense. He did not want Karswell's book in the Museum Society library.

Two days later, Dunning was going home on a tram. He was tired. He looked at the advertisements in the tram – advertisements for soap, chocolate and biscuits. There was a strange notice opposite him. It was written in large blue letters.

IN MEMORY OF JOHN HARRINGTON.
DIED 18TH SEPTEMBER 1899.
HE WAS GIVEN THREE MONTHS TO LIVE.

Dunning touched it. It was part of the window. It was *inside* the glass of the window.

Dunning looked again. The notice had disappeared.

The next day, he was walking along Piccadilly. A man came up to Dunning and gave him a piece of paper. Dunning suddenly felt cold. He looked at the piece of paper. There was a name on it. The name was written in large blue letters.

HARRINGTON

Dunning did not have time to read any more. The man took the paper out of Dunning's hand and ran away. He disappeared into the crowd. Dunning was surprised.

Dunning went into the British Museum Reading Room and sat down at a desk. He took some papers out of his briefcase and started to read.

A large man with a round face walked past the desk. He knocked Dunning's papers onto the floor.

'I am very sorry,' he said and picked up the papers. He handed the papers to Dunning and said, 'These are yours, I believe.'

Dunning was angry. 'Yes, thank you, sir,' he said and took the papers. He suddenly felt cold.

The man with the round face gave an evil smile. He left the Reading Room quickly. Dunning felt unwell and decided to go home.

Mr Farrer, a friend of Dunning, came across the room.

'Are you feeling all right?' he asked.

'No, I'm not feeling well,' Dunning replied.

'What did that man say to you?' Farrer asked. 'Do you know him?'

'No, I don't,' Dunning said.

'That man's name is Karswell,' said Farrer. 'He's an evil man.'

Dunning was surprised.

'Why do you say that?' he asked.

'It's a long story,' Farrer said. 'Let's go and have lunch together.'

Dunning put his papers in his briefcase. The two men left the Reading Room and walked out into the street. Dunning soon felt better.

As they were eating lunch, Farrer told Dunning about Karswell.

'I live near Mr Karswell,' he said. 'Karswell owns a big house with a park, called Lufford Abbey. The village children often played in the park.

'Karswell didn't like children playing in the park. He chased them from the park many times – but they always came back. One day, Karswell invited all the village children to a tea-party. The schoolmaster was very surprised. He took the children to Lufford Abbey after school. Karswell gave a film show.

'The first film showed a wolf with long teeth and sharp claws. Karswell made horrible animal noises and the younger children started to cry.

'Then there was a film about a small boy in a park. It was Lufford Abbey park – where the children liked to play. The boy was followed by a horrible white creature. The boy ran away, but the white creature caught the boy and ate him. The children were all very frightened.

'The children's parents were very angry with the school master and with Karswell,' Farrer went on. 'But Karswell got what he wanted. No children play in Lufford Abbey park any more.'

'How horrible!' said Dunning. Then he asked more slowly, 'Do you, or did you, know Mr John Harrington?'

'You mean John Harrington who died last year?' Farrer asked.

'Yes,' said Dunning. 'Tell me – how did Harrington die?'

'He fell out of a tree,' said Farrer.

'Out of a tree? How strange. What was he doing in a tree?' Dunning asked.

'No one knows,' Farrer said. 'John Harrington was going along a country road late at night. The police said he was running. He dropped his hat and climbed a tree. Then he fell out of the tree and broke his neck.'

'How do you know the story so well?' said Dunning.

'I heard the story from his brother, Henry,' said Farrer. 'You remember Henry Harrington, don't you? You were at university together. Henry lives not far from here – in Piccadilly.'

Dunning went straight home after lunch. He found a note on the door of his house. It was from his doctor.

Dear Dunning,
    Bad news. Both your servants are ill. I believe they ate some bad fish. They are in hospital. Please come to my house.
    Dr Mallows

Dunning went to Dr Mallows's house. The doctor told him what had happened.

'Your servants bought some fish from a man in the street,' the doctor said. 'They told me the man was selling

25

fish to all the houses in the street. It is strange, but no one else is ill.'

Dunning spent the evening at Dr Mallows's house. It was nearly midnight when he went home. He was alone in the house. He went to bed, but he could not sleep. He heard noises – small noises – clocks ticking, doors creaking. He thought he heard noises on the stairs. Was someone coming up the stairs?

He got out of bed and put his ear to the door. He heard nothing.

He opened the door. He stood looking and listening in the dark. A warm wind came into the house. The wind moved past his legs like a cat.

He turned on the light switch. Nothing happened. The electricity was not working.

Dunning kept a candle beside his bed and a box of matches under his pillow. He went to the bed and put his hand under the pillow. He did not feel a box of matches, but he felt a mouth with sharp teeth and fur!

He was so frightened that he ran out of the room. He locked himself in another bedroom. All through the night he listened for noises outside the door. He could not sleep.

In the morning, he opened the door carefully. He looked in his bedroom. He saw nothing unusual. But he was still very frightened. He decided not to stay in the house. He dressed quickly, packed a suitcase, and went to stay at a hotel in Piccadilly.

He sent a message to Mr Henry Harrington. Harrington came to the hotel in the evening. They ate dinner together.

Dunning told Harrington about the strange things that had happened. He asked Henry about his brother – John Harrington.

'My brother,' Harrington began, 'became very strange. For two months, he thought someone was following him. He talked about magic.'

'Magic!' Dunning said in surprise. 'Why did your brother talk about that?'

'John knew a lot about magic,' Harrington said. 'Before his trouble began, John wrote about a book on magic for a newspaper. He said the book was nonsense. The author of the book was very angry. The author's name was Karswell.'

'Karswell!' Dunning said.

'Do you know him?' Harrington asked.

'Yes, I do,' said Dunning. 'He wanted to give a book on magic to the Museum Society. I did not want it in the library. I told him that the book was nonsense.'

'Then you are in danger,' Harrington said. 'I believe that Karswell murdered my brother by magic! I will tell you the whole story.'

The two men finished eating. They sat drinking brandy and smoking cigars.

'Karswell was very angry because John had said the book was nonsense,' Henry Harrington went on. 'Then one evening, something strange happened. John went to a concert. He dropped his programme. A man picked it up and gave it back to him.

'When John came home, he opened the programme. There was a piece of paper inside. Strange red and black letters were written on the paper. John showed it to me.

'This happened last June,' Henry Harrington said. 'The weather was so cold that we had a fire burning. We were looking at the paper when suddenly the door blew open. A warm wind blew into the room. The piece of paper was blown into the fire. It was completely burnt in a moment.'

'A warm wind, on a cold night?' Dunning said.

'Yes, I remember it clearly,' said Harrington. 'It was like something coming into the room. From that night, John had strange dreams. He thought that someone was following him. He didn't want to go out. He kept the lights on in the house and didn't want to be alone.'

'And did you see who was following him?' Dunning asked.

'No, I didn't,' Harrington replied. 'But I saw one other unusual thing. It was a calendar. It came in the post. Every date after 18th September was cut out.'

'And what was the date of the concert?' Dunning asked.

'It was 18th June – three months before my brother died,' Harrington said.

'And your brother died on 18th September, on a country road?' Dunning asked.

'Yes,' said Harrington. 'He was running away from something. The police say he broke his neck when he fell from the tree. But I think he died of fright.'

'But you told me he was afraid to go out of the house,' Dunning said. 'Why was he walking along a country road at night?'

'Because about ten days before he died, the trouble stopped,' Harrington said. 'John felt well. Nothing was following him. He decided to go to the country for a rest.'

'I see,' said Dunning. 'Did your brother think Karswell was making this trouble?'

'Yes, he did,' Harrington replied. 'John remembered Karswell's book on magic. The book told of a way of killing enemies. A magician gives a paper with magic writing on it to his enemy. A devil or demon follows the enemy and kills him.'

'But can the person escape?' Dunning asked.

'Yes, he can,' said Harrington. 'He can escape if he gives the paper back to the magician. My brother couldn't do this because the paper had been burnt. So you must be very careful. You must not take *anything* from Karswell.'

'But I *have*! Dunning said and stood up. 'He handed me my papers in the Museum!'

'Then we must look at those papers immediately,' said Harrington.

The two men went quickly to Dunning's empty house. The servants were still unwell. The electricity was still not working. The house was in darkness. Dunning lit a candle.

He was afraid. He thought that there was someone in the

29

house. Someone was waiting for him.

He opened his briefcase and took out his papers. He had not looked at them since he left the Museum.

He looked through the papers. Suddenly something moved. A piece of paper jumped into the air and flew towards the candle.

Henry Harrington was quick. He caught the paper before it was burnt. He looked at it by the light of the candle. He saw the strange black and red letters.

'Look at the writing,' he said to Dunning. 'It's the same as the writing on the paper given to my brother.'

'What do we do now?' Dunning said.

'We must give the paper back to Karswell,' Harrington said. 'What day did you get it?'

'Yesterday,' Dunning said, '23rd April.'

'Then we have three months,' said Henry. 'We have until 23rd July.'

Harrington paid detectives to watch Karswell. Karswell was in Lufford Abbey. He never came out. The problem was how to get into Lufford Abbey – or how to get Karswell out.

There was no way of getting in. No visitors ever came to Lufford Abbey. They tried to get Karswell out of Lufford Abbey. They sent invitations to Karswell. They put other people's names on the invitations. They invited Karswell to dinners and to meetings. Karswell refused all the invitations. He never left Lufford Abbey.

April passed and so did June and most of July. On 20th July, Dunning knew he was going to die. He wrote letters to his friends and he wrote his will.

That evening a telegram came from the detectives who were watching Karswell's house.

KARSWELL LEAVING VICTORIA STATION
BY BOAT-TRAIN FOR FRANCE
ON THURSDAY NIGHT 22ND JULY.

'Now we can find a way of giving the paper back to Karswell,' Harrington told Dunning. 'We can get on the train and sit near him.'

'But I must give the paper back myself,' said Dunning. 'Karswell knows me. How can I do it?'

'Listen,' said Harrington. 'I have a plan. You must wear a false beard and different clothes. I will get on the train at Victoria Station. I will find Karswell and sit near him.

'The boat-train stops at Croydon. You will get on the train at Croydon and sit near me. We will be on the train together with Karswell. We will find a way of giving him the paper.'

Dunning waited at Croydon railway station. He was worried. The boat-train was late. When the train arrived, Harrington was looking out of a window.

Dunning got on the train. Harrington was sitting in the same carriage as Karswell. Dunning sat down and opened a book. The paper was inside the cover of the book.

Dunning did not look at Harrington. But Karswell looked at both men carefully. Dunning was wearing a false beard and a large hat.

Karswell stood up. He left his coat on the seat. He went out into the corridor to smoke a cigar.

Dunning was going to pick up the coat. But Karswell turned round suddenly. He looked at Dunning very carefully, then sat down again.

The minutes passed. The train was getting nearer and nearer to Dover. Dunning was hot and frightened. How could he give the paper back to Karswell?

The ticket collector came down the corridor. He looked at Dunning's ticket from Croydon. Karswell took out a wallet and showed his ticket. He put the wallet on top of his coat.

Harrington stood up and knocked Karswell's coat onto the floor. Karswell's wallet also fell onto the floor.

'I'm very sorry,' Harrington said and picked up the coat. At the same time, he kicked the wallet towards Dunning. He held out the coat to Karswell and said, 'Here you are.'

Karswell did not take the coat. He looked at Harrington with a look of hate. Dunning picked up the wallet from the floor while Karswell looked at Harrington.

Harrington put the coat down on the seat beside Karswell. Then he turned and showed his ticket to the ticket collector.

As the ticket collector left, Karswell jumped up and followed him.

'Excuse me,' he said, 'can I get a porter at Dover to take my luggage to the boat?'

'Of course, sir,' the ticket collector said. 'We'll be at Dover in five minutes.'

Dunning quickly put the paper in Karswell's wallet. Then he dropped the wallet on the floor.

Karswell came back to the carriage.

'Is this yours, sir?' Dunning asked, picking up the wallet.

Karswell looked at the wallet in Dunning's hand.

'Thank you very much,' he said. And he took the wallet. He did not pick up his coat.

The train slowed down. The carriage became dark. A warm wind started to blow. The train stopped at Dover station. Karswell got off the train as soon as it stopped.

He looked at Harrington with a look of hate.

'Porter!' he shouted. A porter came running. 'Porter, take my luggage and my coat to the ship.'

He looked back at Harrington and gave an evil smile. Then he walked towards the boat.

Dunning and Harrington waited on the platform of the station. The porter took Karswell's luggage to the boat. They heard an officer say, 'I'm sorry, sir, you can't take an animal on the ship.'

Then a moment later,

'I'm sorry, sir. I thought you had an animal with you. I see it's only a coat.'

Karswell got on the ship for France. Dunning and Harrington took the train back to London.

Two days later, a notice appeared in *The Times* newspaper.

THE TIMES

ACCIDENT

Abbeville, France
23rd July 1900

There was an accident today at St Wulfram's Church. An English traveller fell from the church tower. He died immediately. The traveller's name was Mr Karswell, of Lufford Abbey.

THE MAZE

Mr Wilson was a very rich man but he had no children. When he died, he left his house and his money to his nephew, Mr Humphreys. Mr Humphreys was surprised because he had never met his uncle, Mr Wilson.

Mr Humphreys left his job in an office. He went to live in his new house in the country.

Mr Humphreys was shown round the house by Mr Cooper. Mr Cooper was the estate manager. His job was to look after the house and gardens.

'It's a fine house, Mr Humphreys,' said Cooper. 'We all hope you'll be very happy here. The gardens are beautiful. I hope you like gardens, Mr Humphreys?'

'Yes, I do,' said Humphreys, 'very much.'

'Mr Wilson's grandfather started the gardens in 1780,' Cooper said. 'The old gentleman went to Italy and came back with some strange ideas.'

Humphreys looked across the garden.

'I see there is a Roman temple,' he said.

'Yes, sir, there is,' said Cooper. 'Shall we go and look at it?'

The two men walked through the beautiful, large gardens. There were many paths with trees and bushes on either side. The Roman temple was on top of a small hill. There was a pile of stone blocks inside the temple.

'What are these stone blocks for?' Humphreys asked.

'I don't know, sir,' said Cooper. 'They came out of the maze.'

'The maze?' said Humphreys. 'I didn't know there was a maze in the gardens. Did Mr Wilson make it?'

'No, he didn't, sir,' said Cooper. 'Mr Wilson's grandfather planted the trees for the maze. Mr Wilson never went in there. He didn't let anyone else go in either. Twenty years ago, Mr Wilson gave orders for these stones to be taken out of the maze. Then the gate to the maze was locked. No one has been in there since.'

Mr Humphreys looked at the stone blocks. Each one had a letter cut into it.

'How interesting,' he said. 'I want to look at this maze.'

'It's over there, sir,' said Cooper, pointing to a small wood. 'There's a wall around it and the gate's locked. I'll go to the house and get the key.'

Cooper went back to the house. Humphreys walked to the small wood. He found a wall with a gate.

The gate was locked with an old padlock. Above the gate was some writing in Latin – SECRETUM MEUM MIHI ET FILIIS DOMUS MEAE.

'Let me see,' Humphreys said. 'That means something like – "My secret is for me and for the sons of my house." Well, I'm a son of the house. The secret is mine too!'

He kicked the old padlock. It broke and fell to the ground. He opened the gate and went into the maze.

A dark path led into the maze. Inside, paths ran between thick hedges of tall yew trees.

It was difficult to walk along the paths. The branches of the trees had grown across the paths. They almost blocked the way. Humphreys was the first person to walk in the maze for twenty years.

He walked to the centre of the maze without getting lost.

This is too easy, he said to himself. A maze is a puzzle. People always get lost in a maze.

A stone column stood in the centre of the maze. It was about four feet high. On top of the column, there was a metal globe. There were drawings and writing on the globe.

A stone column stood in the centre of the maze.

It was dark and hot in the maze. There was no wind. There was a strange silence. Humphreys noticed that the birds had stopped singing.

He turned to go. Then he heard something moving in the maze behind him. He looked round. He was suddenly afraid. He thought that someone was watching him.

'Ah, there you are,' said Cooper, coming round a corner. 'I followed your footprints in the dead leaves. I see you didn't need the key.'

Humphreys was pleased to see Cooper. He thought he was going to see someone or something else.

The two men walked back to the house.

'Can you ask the gardeners to clear the paths,' said Humphreys. 'Tell me, why did Mr Wilson close the maze?'

'I'm not sure, sir,' Cooper replied. 'Mr Wilson didn't like his grandfather – old Mr Wilson – the one who planted the maze. He burnt all his grandfather's books. Perhaps that is why he closed the maze.'

'What do you know about old Mr Wilson?' Humphreys asked.

'Not much, sir,' said Cooper. 'He's been dead for fifty years. No one knows where he's buried. He had an Italian servant. The Italian servant buried his master at night. He was buried somewhere here in the gardens. But the grave has never been found.'

'How very strange!' said Humphreys.

Mr Humphreys went back to the house. A letter was waiting for him.

> *Bentley Manor*
> *14th August 1880*
>
> *Dear Mr. Humphreys,*
>
> *You don't know me but I am your neighbour I am writing a book on English gardens. May I visit your garden? I am interested in the maze. I asked your uncle many times to let me see the maze. But he never let me see it. I hope you will let me see it. Also, I'd like to have a plan of the maze. I hope this is possible.*
>
> > *Your neighbour,*
> > *Lady Wardrop*

Mr Humphreys immediately replied to Lady Wardrop's letter. He invited her to visit the gardens the next day. He promised to give her a plan of the maze.

I shall draw a plan tomorrow morning, he said to himself.

He spent the evening in the library. There were thousands of books. He saw a very thin book on a high shelf. It was called *The Secret of the Maze*. He took the book to his bedroom. He wanted to read it before he fell asleep.

He looked out of the bedroom window. There was a bright moon in the sky. The gardens were beautiful in the moonlight. White moonlight shone on the Roman temple. There was a red light in the maze. Something was burning.

Of course, Humphreys said to himself. The gardeners cleared leaves from the paths of the maze this afternoon. They lit a fire to burn all the dead wood and leaves. The fire is still burning.

There was one strange thing Mr Humphreys did not like about the gardens. There was one yew tree growing alone. It stood half-way between the maze and the house.

'I haven't seen that tree before,' Humphreys said. 'It's in a strange place. I will tell the gardeners to cut it down.' Then he started to read the small book called *The Secret of the Maze*.

There was a story in the book about a maze. The story happened many, many years ago. The maze was in a strange land. At the centre of the maze, there was a red jewel. The jewel was very valuable.

Many men tried to find the jewel. Many men went into the maze, but no one ever came out again.

One day, a traveller went into the maze. He saw the pathways clearly. The sun was shining. The traveller found the centre of the maze by the end of the day. The red jewel was at the centre of the maze. The jewel was the colour of fire.

A voice spoke to the traveller, 'You have learnt the secret of the maze.'

A doorway opened to a beautiful garden. The voice said, 'This is the Garden of Peace. You may go in, but you may never leave the Garden again. Choose between the Garden and the jewel. You cannot have both.'

The traveller wanted to be a rich man. So he took the jewel and the garden disappeared. The traveller tried to find the path out of the maze. But he got lost. Night fell. The creatures of the night came out of the ground. They had no eyes, but they could smell the traveller. They had sharp teeth and claws. They were hungry for flesh and blood!

The traveller ran along the dark pathways. The night creatures followed him. All night, the traveller ran through the maze. All night, the creatures followed him.

In the morning, the night creatures disappeared back into the ground. Daylight came, but no sun. A thick, white mist covered the maze.

40

The tired traveller walked round the maze. At last he came to the gate. The gate was locked. Above the gate, there was a sign – "No man may go out of this gate unless another man comes in".

The traveller called through the gate to the people outside, 'Come in and let me out! I know the secret of the maze. I have the jewel. Come in here and I will make you rich! But no one came.

Humphreys put the book down and fell asleep. He started to dream. He was afraid. He was not in his bed. He was standing inside a gate. He was holding something in his hand. It was hot and red. It shone with a red light. There was a white mist all around him. He was calling out loudly, 'Help me! Help me! Open the gate!'

A face appeared at the gate. He thought he knew the person's face. The person smiled. He was opening the gate. Humphreys felt happy.

Free! he thought, free at last!

Then he looked at the man who was opening the gate. He knew the man's face. It was himself!

'No! No!' Humphreys cried out and woke up. He was on the floor beside his bed. The book he had been reading was gone. It was never found again.

After breakfast, Humphreys took some paper and a pen. He went out into the garden.

I will draw a plan of the maze, he said to himself.

Once again, he walked straight to the centre of the maze. He did not get lost.

The gardeners had done their job well. The pathways were clear. The gardeners had also cleaned the metal globe.

Humphreys looked at the globe carefully. A strange creature was drawn round the centre of the globe. The

'Help me! Help me! Open the gate!'

words – UMBRA MORTIS – 'the shadow of death' were written below the creature. The creature was eating its own tail. Above the creature was a man with wings. The man's head was hidden by a ring at the top of the globe. Around the ring was written – PRINCEPS TENEBRARUM – 'the Prince of Darkness'.

The globe was very strange. Perhaps old Mr Wilson had brought it back from Italy.

Humphreys knocked on the metal globe with his hand. The metal did not seem very thick. The globe sounded hollow.

Humphreys was surprised. The globe was hot! It burnt his hand. Was something burning inside the metal globe?

He walked away from the globe. He started to draw a plan of the maze. It was difficult and he made mistakes. Then it started to rain. Humphreys stopped drawing and went back to the house.

In the afternoon, the rain stopped. Soon after lunch, Lady Wardrop arrived.

'It is very kind of you to let me see your gardens,' Lady Wardrop said. 'Tell me, do you have a plan of your maze?'

'I started to draw one this morning,' Humphreys said.

'Oh good,' Lady Wardrop said. 'Could you let me have a copy for my book?'

Lady Wardrop talked about gardens. She had visited all the famous gardens in England. Humphreys listened politely and led her to the entrance of the maze.

'Do you know the way to the centre of the maze?' asked Lady Wardrop.

'Certainly,' said Humphreys. 'Please follow me.'

They walked around inside the maze for a quarter of an hour. They walked round and round in circles. Mr

Humphreys could not find the centre of the maze.

'I am very sorry, Lady Wardrop,' he said. 'I was sure I knew the way. I've walked to the centre twice before without making a mistake.'

Lady Wardrop was hot and red in the face. 'I've seen many mazes,' she said, 'but not one like this. It makes me feel strange.'

'Why?' Humphreys asked.

'Look,' said Lady Wardrop, pointing to a tree. 'Here's my handkerchief. We came along here five minutes ago. I put my handkerchief on a tree on the right-hand side of the path. Now we've come this way again. But my handkerchief is on the left-hand side.'

'That's because we've come from the other direction,' Humphreys said.

'I'm not so sure,' Lady Wardrop said. 'Also, have you noticed those holes in the ground? There is one on the left-hand side of each corner.'

'Those are probably where the stone blocks came from,' said Humphreys. 'We're near the gate. Shall we leave the maze and I'll show you the stone blocks?'

He took Lady Wardrop to the Roman temple. He showed her the stone blocks.

'Mr Wilson took them out of the maze,' he said. 'Each block has a letter cut into it.'

'That is probably the answer to the puzzle of the maze,' said Lady Wardrop. 'Put the letters together and they will spell words. When the stones were in their holes, you followed the words to find the centre of the maze. But, of course, you had to know the words – that was the secret.'

'Ah, very simple!' said Humphreys as they walked back to the house. 'I will let you have a plan of the maze very soon.'

'Thank you very much,' said Lady Wardrop. 'Use string.'

'String? What do you mean?' Humphreys asked.

'Tie a ball of string to the gate,' said Lady Wardrop. 'Take the ball of string with you as you go through the maze. Then you can't get lost.'

'What a good idea,' said Humphreys.

Humphreys went to bed early, but did not read. He did not want any more bad dreams.

He looked out of the window. He remembered the yew tree growing near the house. But he was mistaken. There was no yew tree. He looked all around. The only yew tree he could see was outside the library. He had not seen it before.

The next morning, he took paper and pencils and a ball of string into the gardens. He walked straight to the centre of the maze. How did I get lost yesterday? he asked himself.

He tied the ball of string to the metal globe. Then he walked back to the gate carrying the ball of string. The string went from the centre of the maze to the entrance.

Now it was easy to draw a plan. But it took him all day. He finished in the late afternoon and went back to the house for tea. There was a note from Lady Wardrop.

16th August

Dear Mr. Humphreys,

Thank you for showing me the maze. You won't forget to give me a plan, will you? Have you looked underneath the stone blocks? Have they got numbers on them?

Yours sincerely,
Lady Wardrop

Humphreys decided to look at the stone blocks again the next day.

The evening was very hot. He opened all the windows.

That yew tree outside the library window will have to be cut down, he thought. It shuts out the light. And the branches are growing everywhere. Some of them are coming into the room.

He sat down and started to draw the plan of the maze. He worked until nearly midnight.

From time to time, he looked at the window. He thought that there was someone outside. He felt someone was waiting to come in. But there was no one there. It was only the yew tree.

He drew the last lines of his plan. As he finished, he saw a black mark on the paper in the centre of the plan.

He looked at the mark. But it was not a mark on the paper. It was a hole.

Humphreys saw the black hole becoming larger and larger. He looked down into the hole. There was something at the bottom of the hole. Something was coming up and up.

Humphreys could not move.

He looked at the thing that was coming nearer and nearer. It was grey and black. It was a ball with two holes for eyes. It came nearer and Humphreys saw a face. It was a horribly burnt face!

The thing reached out two black arms to pull Humphreys down into the hole.

Humphreys screamed. He threw himself backwards. He tried to get away from the burnt face and arms. He cried out as he hit his head on the wall.

Then everything went black.

A doctor came to see Mr Humphreys.

'Mr Humphreys needs a long rest,' the doctor told Mr Cooper. 'He is speaking very strangely. He is talking about some stones in a Roman temple. He wants you to go and look at them. He wants to know if there are numbers on them. Mr Humphreys wants to know if the letters on the blocks spell words.

'Also, he wants you to open the metal globe in the centre of the maze,' the doctor went on. 'After that, he wants you to cut down the maze and burn the trees.'

Lady Wardrop came to the house when she heard of Mr Humphreys' illness. The gardeners were busy cutting down the maze and burning the yew trees.

Cooper came up to her and said, 'Excuse me, Lady Wardrop, but we've got two strange things here. Shall I show them to Mr Humphreys?'

'Let me see them,' said Lady Wardrop.

The first thing was a broken metal globe. Inside the globe, was the burnt body of a man.

'We think it's the body of old Mr Wilson,' said Cooper. 'We never found out where he was buried.'

The second thing which Cooper showed Lady Wardrop was a row of stone blocks. They were lying outside the Roman temple.

'There was a number on the bottom of each block,' said Cooper. 'I put them in order. I'm afraid I don't know much Latin, Lady Wardrop. Can you tell us what it means?'

The words on the blocks said – PENETRANS AD INTERIORA MORTIS.

'I think it means – "The path to the centre of death" ,' said Lady Wardrop.

THE LOST CROWNS OF ANGLIA

Seaburgh is a small town by the sea on the east coast of England. This part of England is called East Anglia. I went to Seaburgh for a holiday in 1919 with my friend, Henry Long.

There were few visitors in Seaburgh that year. There was only one other visitor in our hotel. His name was Paxton. Paxton was a tall, thin young man. He looked worried and unhappy.

One evening, when Henry and I were sitting in the hotel lounge, Paxton came up to us.

'Excuse me,' said Paxton, 'I must speak to somebody. Something strange has happened to me. I'd like to talk to someone about it. May I talk to you?'

'Of course,' I said. 'Please sit down and tell us about it.'

'A few days ago,' Paxton said, 'I went for a walk to Freston. Freston is a village about five miles from here. I took my camera with me. The church at Freston has an unusual door. I wanted to photograph it. There are three wooden crowns on the door.

'The village priest came out of the church. I asked him about the three crowns on the door. The priest told me a strange story.

'Many years ago,' said Paxton, 'Anglia was a kingdom. The last king of Anglia died over a thousand years ago. When he died, his three crowns disappeared. The people believed that the crowns were magic. They believed that the crowns were buried in different places. The crowns guarded the coast against enemies from across the sea.

'About three hundred years ago, one of the crowns was found. It was secretly sold – no one knows what happened to it after that.'

'What about the other two crowns?' asked Henry.

'The second crown was washed into the sea. It was never found again.'

'What about the third crown?' I asked Paxton. 'Was it ever found?'

'I'll tell you about that,' answered Paxton. 'There was a family here called Ager. The people believed that the Agers were guardians of the third crown. The last Ager died a year ago, in 1918. He had no children. I found his grave in the churchyard – I wrote down what was written on the gravestone.

WILLIAM AGER
died
21st December 1918
aged
28 years

'Later, I went to the bookshop in Freston. By chance, I found an old book dated 1740. Inside it were some lines of poetry:

> *'Nathaniel Ager is my name,*
> *I own the hill above the sand,*
> *All Agers' duty is the same:*
> *To guard the crown that guards the land.*
>
> *When I am dead and in my grave,*
> *And all my bones are rotten,*
> *My sons shall keep my name alive:*
> *It shall not be forgotten.'*

'I bought the book and walked back towards Seaburgh. I found the house where William Ager had lived. The house is half-way between Freston and Seaburgh.

'Above the house is a small hill. There is a circle of trees on top. I knew that this was the place!'

'The place for what?' I asked. Henry and I were becoming tired of this long story.

'The place where the crown was buried,' said Paxton.

'And did you find this crown?' I asked in a tired voice.

Paxton's answer surprised us both.

'I have it in my room,' he said. 'Come and see it, then you'll believe me.'

Henry and I did not believe him. We thought that Paxton was not telling the truth. But we stood up and followed him.

Paxton led us to his room. He opened a suitcase. Inside the suitcase was something wrapped in newspapers. He unwrapped the newspapers. There was a crown!

The crown was made of silver. It was a circle of metal with four jewels. I put out my hand to touch it.

'Don't touch it!' Paxton cried and held the crown away from us.

'Why not?' I asked in surprise. 'We won't take it from you!'

'I'm sorry,' said Paxton. 'It's because . . .' He looked round the room in a strange way. 'Since I took the crown, I haven't been alone.'

'You haven't been alone?' Henry said. 'What do you mean?'

Then Paxton told us more of his story.

'After I'd been to Ager's house, I came back here. I got a spade and a lantern. When it was dark, I went back to the hill above the house. I started to dig a hole at the top of the hill, in the centre of the circle of trees.

'As I was digging,' Paxton went on, 'I was sure someone was watching me. Once, I thought I saw someone. But I wasn't sure. The person was always behind me.

'Once, I felt someone pulling my coat. But then I found the crown. At that moment, I heard a terrible cry behind me.'

'Who cried out?' I asked.

'I couldn't see anyone,' Paxton answered. 'But I think I know.' He pointed to a book on a table beside the bed. 'Every time I come back to my room the old book is open.'

I looked at the table. The old book was open at the first page. I saw the name – William Ager 1890.

'So you think that William Ager is following you?' I said. 'But William Ager is dead.'

'It's the ghost of William Ager,' said Paxton. 'He won't leave me alone. He wants the crown, but he isn't strong enough to take it from me.'

'And what will you do with the crown?' I asked.

'I'm going to put it back,' said Paxton.

'If you put it back, will William Ager's ghost leave you alone?' I asked.

'I don't know,' said Paxton. 'But I must try.'

I saw that Paxton was very, very frightened.

'Then we shall help you put it back tonight,' I said.

As I spoke, a shadow moved in the room. Paxton saw it and looked terrified.

That night, as we left the hotel together, I spoke to the hotel porter.

'It's a warm night,' I said. 'We're going for a walk. We may be back very late.'

'I'll wait for you, sir,' said the porter. 'I won't lock the front door until you return. The other gentleman isn't staying in the hotel, is he?'

'I heard a terrible cry behind me.'

'What other gentleman?' I asked.

'The gentleman who's with Mr Paxton,' said the porter.

'No,' I replied quickly. I did not tell the others what the porter had said. But I had seen it too. When the three of us were together, I thought I saw another person in the room with us.

It took us half an hour to walk to William Ager's house. The road went along beside the beach. The beach was a lonely place at night.

We saw the hill above the beach. The sea was calm. The moon was shining behind the trees on the hill.

We climbed to the top of the hill. We had forgotten to bring a spade. Paxton did not care. He began to dig with his hands.

As soon as he had dug the hole, Paxton put the crown in it. He covered the crown with earth.

'It's back,' he said in a loud voice. 'Will you leave me in peace now, William Ager?'

We heard nothing. But Paxton turned to us and said, 'William Ager says – "Never!"'

We took Paxton back to the hotel. He walked in silence, looking down at the ground.

'Don't worry,' I said. 'Everything will be all right tomorrow. We'll put you on a train to London. As soon as you are on the train you will forget all about this.'

'He'll never let me go,' Paxton said.

The next morning, Henry knocked on my door before seven o'clock.

'Let's go and have breakfast,' he said. 'Then we'll take Paxton to the railway station.'

I got dressed and went downstairs. Henry was waiting for me.

'Have you seen Paxton?' I asked Henry.

'He's not in his room,' he said. 'I thought he was with you!'

We went quickly to the porter.

'Have you seen Mr Paxton this morning?' I asked.

'Yes, sir,' said the porter. 'He went out a couple of minutes ago. In fact, I thought he was with you, sir.'

'With *me*?' I asked in surprise.

'Yes, sir,' the porter said. 'I thought you were outside the hotel, calling for him. It *looked* like you, sir. But I was reading the paper.

'Something strange happened at Freston yesterday.'

'What happened?' I asked.

'A grave was opened at the church,' the porter said. 'The body's disappeared.'

'Whose grave was opened?' I asked.

'A man who used to live here,' the porter replied. 'A strange man, called William Ager.'

Henry and I ran outside. Paxton was on the beach. He was walking quickly and waving to someone. We could not see who he was waving to. There was a thick mist coming from the sea.

As we ran after Paxton, the mist became thicker. In a few seconds, we could not see Paxton. But we saw his footprints in the wet sand. The marks of his shoes were clear.

There were other marks in the sand. They were made by someone who was not wearing shoes. The marks were strange. They were the shape of feet. But they were feet without flesh – only bone.

We called Paxton's name. We thought we heard Paxton call our names. Then we heard a long and horrible scream. I shall never forget the sound of that scream in the mist.

We stopped. We were afraid. We did not want to meet the creature that Paxton had met. We both knew that Paxton was dead.

We walked forward slowly. A few yards away, we found Paxton's body. His mouth was full of sand and stones. His neck was broken.

We heard a strange laugh in the mist. It was not the laugh of a living man. Henry and I were terribly afraid.

The police asked us a lot of questions. They never found out who murdered poor Mr Paxton. Henry and I did not tell the police what we knew. They would not have believed us.

Henry and I did not go back to look for the crown of Anglia. The crown is safe. We did not want to meet the ghost of the guardian – William Ager.

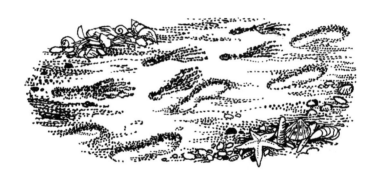

Points for Understanding

1 Why did Mr Anderson go to Viborg?
2 Mr Anderson stayed in the Golden Lion Inn.
   (a) How old was the inn?
   (b) Which two rooms did the landlord show him?
   (c) Which room did Mr Anderson choose?
3 What happened when Anderson tried to open his bedroom door that evening?
4 What did Anderson think when he lit the oil-lamp in room 12?
5 Why did the townspeople of Viborg want Francken to leave the city?
6 What did Anderson hear when he stopped outside the door of room 13?
7 What had disappeared from room 12?
8 Anderson went to the window and lit a cigarette.
   (a) How many shadows did Anderson see on the wall opposite?
   (b) What was strange about the shadow from room 13?
9 Where were Anderson's suitcase and ashtray in the morning?
10 Why did Anderson think he was going mad?
11 'Who is in room 13?' Anderson asked the landlord. What did the landlord reply?
12 In the evening, Anderson invited the landlord to his room. What happened when they were in room 12?
13 Why did Anderson shout and pull Jensen away from the door of room 13?
14 What happened when the men swung their axes at the door of room 13?
15 A box of old papers was found under the floor of room 13. Who did Anderson think the papers had belonged to?
16 Many people believe that some numbers are magical or unlucky. Are there any special numbers in your country? What are they?

THE WHISTLE

1 Parkins stayed at the Globe Inn in Burnstow.
    (a) How many rooms were there in the inn?
    (b) How many beds were there in Parkins' room?
    (c) What was unusual about the window?
2 Where had Colonel Wilson lived for many years?
3 What is an archeologist?
4 Why did Parkins not walk back to the inn with the Colonel?
5 What did Parkins find in the hole?
6 Why did Professor Parkins suddenly feel afraid?
7 What was written on the whistle? What happened when the Professor blew the whistle?
8 What did Parkins see in his dream?
9 In the morning, the servant came to clean Parkins' room. What was strange about the beds?
10 What did the boy see in the window of Parkins' room?
11 What did the Colonel tell Parkins to do with the whistle?
12 'A noise came from the empty bed.'
    (a) What did Parkins see on the bed?
    (b) What did the face under the sheet look like?
    (c) Who came into the room?
13 Why is the Professor afraid of curtains that move in the wind?

THE MESSAGE OF DEATH

1 Why did Dunning not want Karswell's book in the Museum Society library?
2 What was the strange notice Dunning saw in the tram window?
3 A man handed Dunning a piece of paper. What was written on the paper?
4 A man knocked Dunning's papers off his desk. What happened when the man gave the papers back to Dunning?
5 Farrer said Karswell was an evil man. What had Karswell done to the village children?
6 How did John Harrington die?
7 What had happened to Dunning's servants?

8 Dunning stayed one night in the empty house. In the morning, he went to stay at a hotel. Why?

9 How had John Harrington made Karswell angry?

10 John Harrington found a piece of paper in his programme when he came back from the concert.
    (a) What was written on the paper?
    (b) What happened to the piece of paper?

11 'You must not take anything from Karswell,' Henry Harrington told Dunning. Why? What had Dunning taken from Karswell?

12 How did Henry Harrington stop the piece of paper being burnt?

13 What must Dunning do to stay alive?

14 A telegram came from the detectives who were watching Karswell.
    (a) Where was Karswell going?
    (b) Which train was he going on?
    (c) What was Harrington's plan?

15 How did Dunning hand the paper back to Karswell?

16 A notice appeared in *The Times* newspaper. What did the notice say?

THE MAZE

1 Why was Mr Humphreys able to leave work?

2 Who was Mr Cooper?

3 Who had started the gardens?

4 What did Mr Humphreys see in the Roman temple?

5 Who planted the trees for the maze?

6 Why was the gate to the maze always locked?

7 Mr Wilson had given orders about the stones in the maze. What were the orders?

8 What was written above the door of the maze?

9 Why did Mr Humphreys think the maze was too easy?

10 What was on top of the stone column in the centre of the maze?

11 Why did Mr Humphreys suddenly feel afraid?

12 Where was old Mr Wilson buried?

13 Who wanted to come and see the gardens?

14 What book did Mr Humphreys find in the library?

15 Mr Humphreys looked out of the window before he went to bed.
    (a) What did he see in the maze?
    (b) What did he think it was?
    (c) What strange thing did Mr Humphreys see in the gardens?
16 Mr Humphreys read a story in the book called *The Secret of the Maze*. What was in the centre of the maze? Did the traveller find the centre of the maze?
17 In the story, the traveller heard a voice.
    (a) What did the voice say?
    (b) What did the traveller choose?
    (c) Did the traveller ever get out of the maze?
18 Mr Humphreys had a dream. Where was he? Who came to help him in his dream?
19 Next morning, Mr Humphreys examined the globe carefully.
    (a) What was drawn round the centre of the globe?
    (b) What was written on the globe?
20 What happened when Mr Humphreys tried to take Lady Wardrop to the centre of the maze?
21 Why did Lady Wardrop want to know if the stones in the Roman temple were numbered?
22 What was growing outside the library window?
23 Mr Humphreys saw a black mark in the centre of the plan.
    (a) What happened when he looked down at the mark?
    (b) What was coming up out of the hole?
24 The doctor told Cooper that Mr Humphreys was speaking very strangely.
    (a) What did Mr Humphreys want to know about the stones in the Roman temple?
    (b) What did he want Cooper to do to the metal globe and the trees of the maze?
25 What did the gardeners find in the metal globe?
26 There were letters on the stones. The letters made a message in Latin. What did Lady Wardrop say the words meant?

THE LOST CROWNS OF ANGLIA

1 Where is Seaburgh?
2 How many guests were in the hotel?
3 Why did Paxton want to talk to someone?
4 What happened to the three crowns of Anglia when the king died?
5 What did people believe about the crowns?
6 What did people believe about the family called Ager?
7 When did the last person in the Ager family die? Where was he buried?
8 Why did Paxton feel strange when he was digging?
9 What was Paxton going to do with the crown?
10 How many people did the porter think were with Paxton?
11 Paxton put the crown back in the ground.
    (a) What question did he ask in a loud voice?
    (b) What answer did he get to his question?
12 What did Paxton do early in the morning?
13 What had happened at Freston the day before? How do we know this?
14 They saw Paxton's footsteps in the sand. What other marks did they see?
15 What happened to Paxton?
16 Why did Henry and the Storyteller not tell the police what they had seen?
17 Why did they not go back to find the crown?

ELEMENTARY LEVEL

Road to Nowhere *by John Milne*
The Black Cat *by John Milne*
Don't Tell Me What To Do *by Michael Hardcastle*
The Runaways *by Victor Canning*
The Red Pony *by John Steinbeck*
The Goalkeeper's Revenge and Other Stories *by Bill Naughton*
The Stranger *by Norman Whitney*
The Promise *by R.L. Scott-Buccleuch*
The Man With No Name *by Evelyn Davies and Peter Town*
The Cleverest Person in the World *by Norman Whitney*
Claws *by John Landon*
Z for Zachariah *by Robert C. O'Brien*
Tales of Horror *by Bram Stoker*
Frankenstein *by Mary Shelley*
Silver Blaze and Other Stories *by Sir Arthur Conan Doyle*
Tales of Ten Worlds *by Arthur C. Clarke*
The Boy Who Was Afraid *by Armstrong Sperry*
Room 13 and Other Ghost Stories *by M.R. James*
The Narrow Path *by Francis Selormey*
The Woman in Black *by Susan Hill*

For further information on the full selection of
Readers at all five levels in the series, please refer
to the Heinemann Readers catalogue.

Published by Macmillan Heinemann ELT
Between Towns Road, Oxford OX4 3PP
Macmillan Heinemann ELT is an imprint of
Macmillan Publishers Limited
Companies and representatives throughout the world

ISBN 0 435 27192 X

This retold version by Stephen Colbourn for Macmillan Guided Readers
First published 1989
Design and illustration © Macmillan Publishers Limited 2002
Heinemann is a registered trademark of Reed Educational & Professional Publishing Limited
This version first published 2002

Illustrated by Alan Burton
Cover by Simon Noyes and Threefold Design

Printed in China

2006 2005 2004 2003 2002
19 18 17 16 15 14 13 12 11